This Lollipop and Grandpa Book

Belongs to:

· ·

For Pete, the boy who always wanted to be a dentist. PH

For my Mum. CJ

Lollipop and Grandpa and the Wobbly Tooth

ISBN: 978-1-907912-14-6

Published in Great Britain by Phoenix Yard Books Ltd

This edition published 2012

Phoenix Yard Books
Phoenix Yard
65 King's Cross Road
London
WC1X 9LW

Text copyright © Penelope Harper, 2012

Illustrations copyright © Cate James, 2012

1 3 5 7 9 10 8 6 4 2

Book design by Insight Design Concepts

Printed in Singapore

A CIP catalogue record for this book is available from
the British Library

www.phoenixyardbooks.com

Lollipop
and
Grandpa
and the
Wobbly Tooth

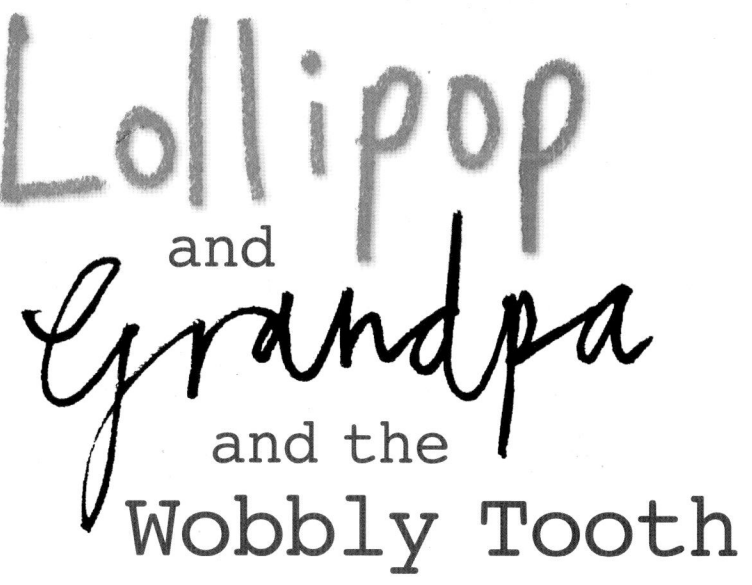

Penelope Harper
Illustrated by Cate James

Lollipop has a beautiful set of teeth.
She brushes them every morning...

and she brushes them every night.

She loves to show them to people by
grinning the widest possible grin.

Lollipop grins a lot when Grandpa
comes to visit.

Grandpa grins a lot too, but his smile is very funny.
He has a few gaps that he can suck soup through.

It makes Mum cross, but it
makes Lollipop giggle.

slurrrrrp
slurrrrrp
slurrrrrp

Grandpa says he has gaps because, when he was little, people didn't look after their teeth very well.

"That's alright," says Lollipop, "I take really good care of my teeth."

Grandpa tells Lollipop that one day her baby teeth will drop out, and big, bright, brand new teeth will grow in their place.

Lollipop wonders if they will be **big teeth,** like a rabbit...

or even **bigger teeth,** like a walrus...

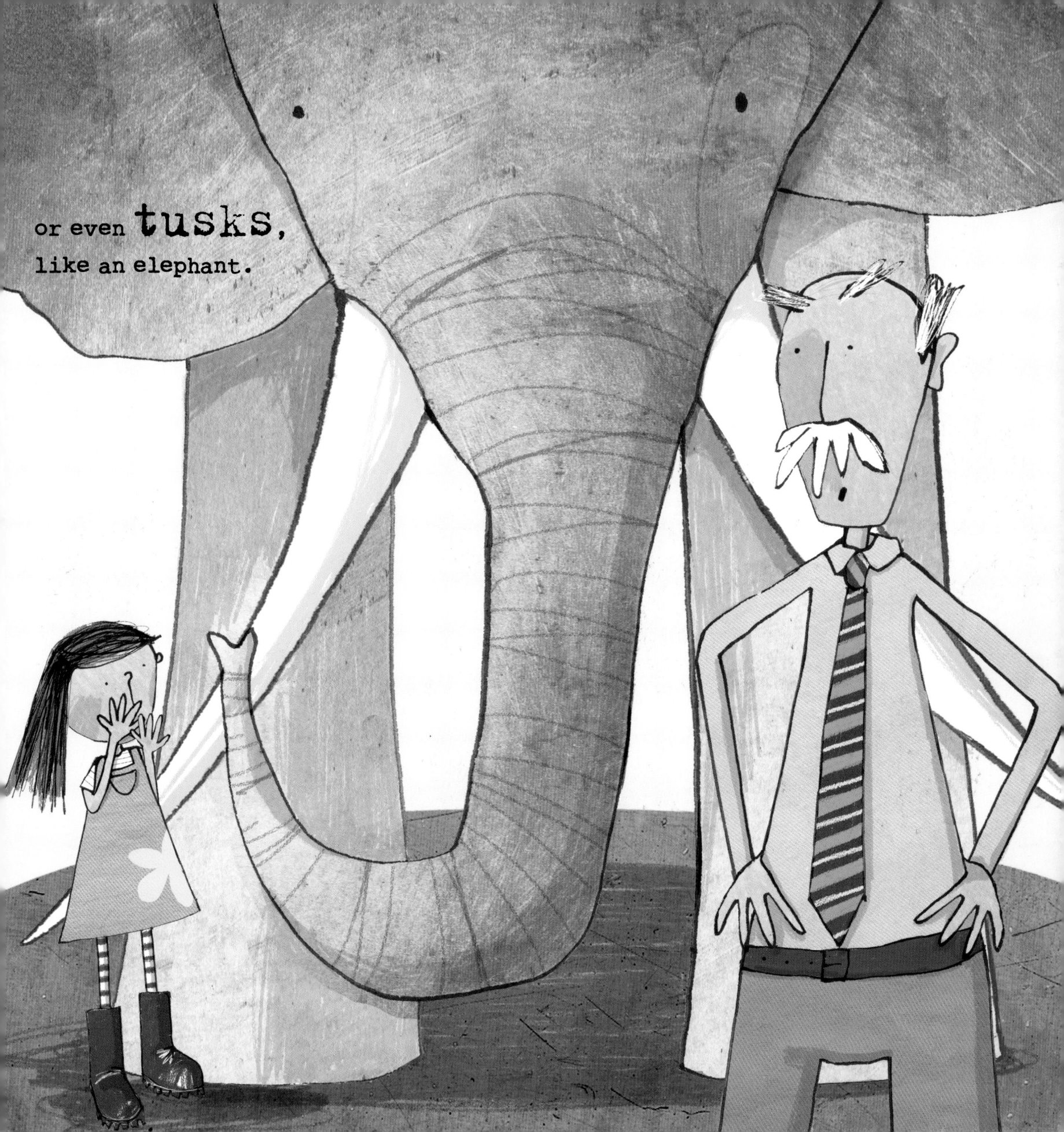

or even **tusks**,
like an elephant.

One morning,
Lollipop runs
her tongue over
her sparkling,
shiny teeth.

There's a
wibble...

then a
wobble...

"GRANDPA!

Look, Grandpa!
I have a wobbly tooth!"
shouts Lollipop.

"A wobbly tooth?" cries Grandpa. "A wibbly-wobbly, bibbly-bobbly tooth that's coming loose?"
"What do we do?" asks Lollipop.

"Right!" cries Grandpa, leaping up. "We need a plan of action to fix that wobbly tooth."

Lollipop is a little bit worried about what Grandpa has in mind. "Do you mean glue it back in, or p-p-pull it out?" she asks. "Precisely," says Grandpa.

"We'll **PULL** it out!
We'll go down to the fair today and wait until
they have the tug of war competition.
The referee will shout,

"TUUUUUUUUUUUUUUUUUUUUG!"

Lollipop looks at Grandpa with her mouth wide open.
"B-but what happens if the loose tooth doesn't come out,
and I just get...

SQUISHED?" she cries.

Lollipop is not certain Grandpa has thought this through.

"Well, perhaps if we can't **PULL** it out, then we can **KNOCK** it out.

There's a big woodpecker that lives in my garden.
He goes tap tap tap on the trees to try and find insects.
We can climb the tree, and he can **tap tap tap**
on the tooth until it drops out."

Lollipop's mouth is even wider now.

"But what happens if he **tap tap taps** the tooth too much, and I fall out of the tree?"

THUD!

Grandpa is running out of ideas.
He scratches his head and has a think.

Suddenly Grandpa shouts, "EUREKA!

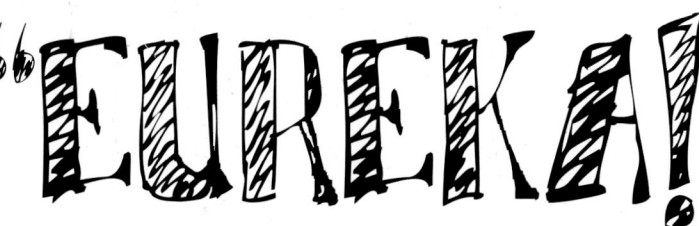

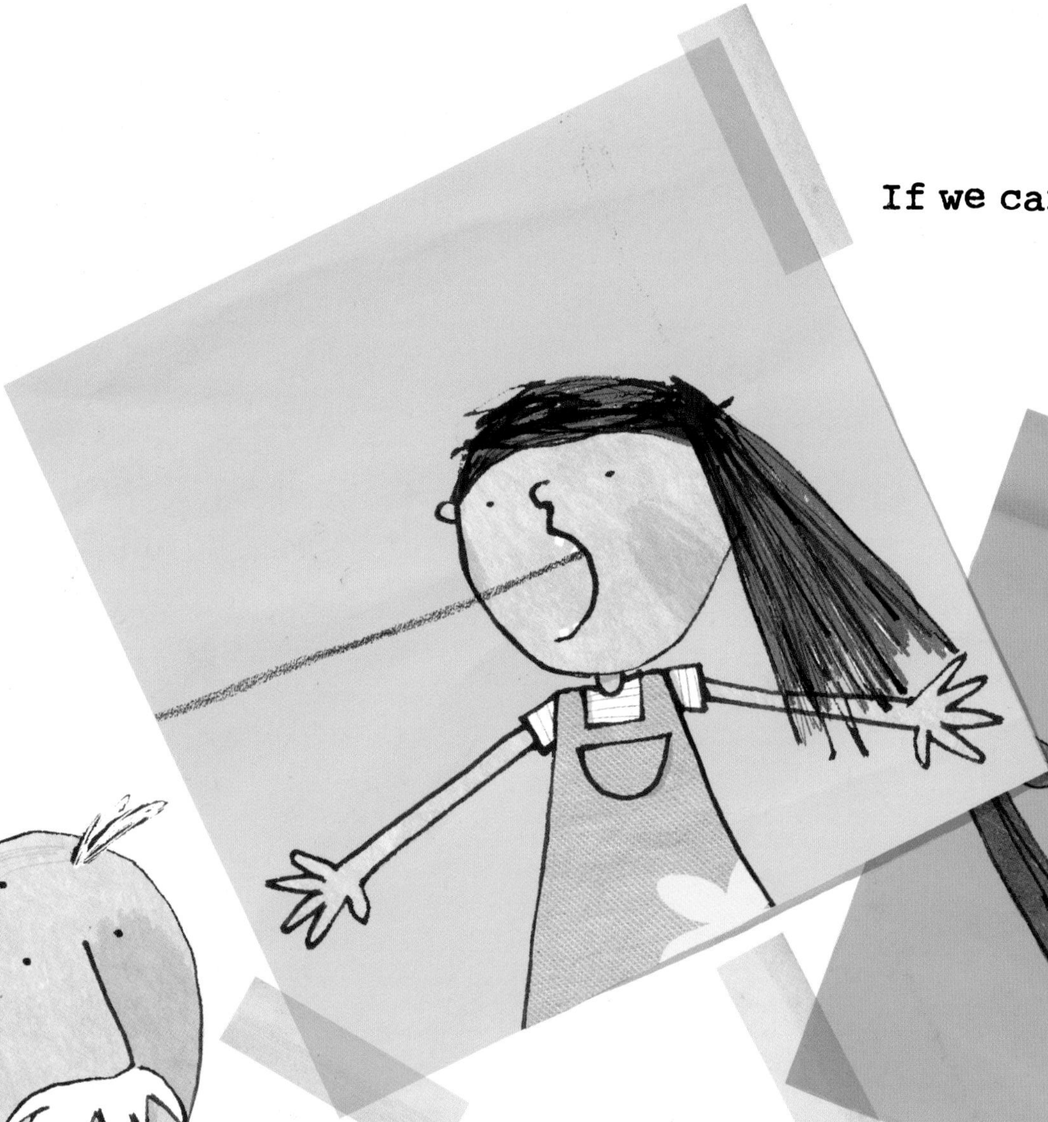

If we can't **PULL** it out...

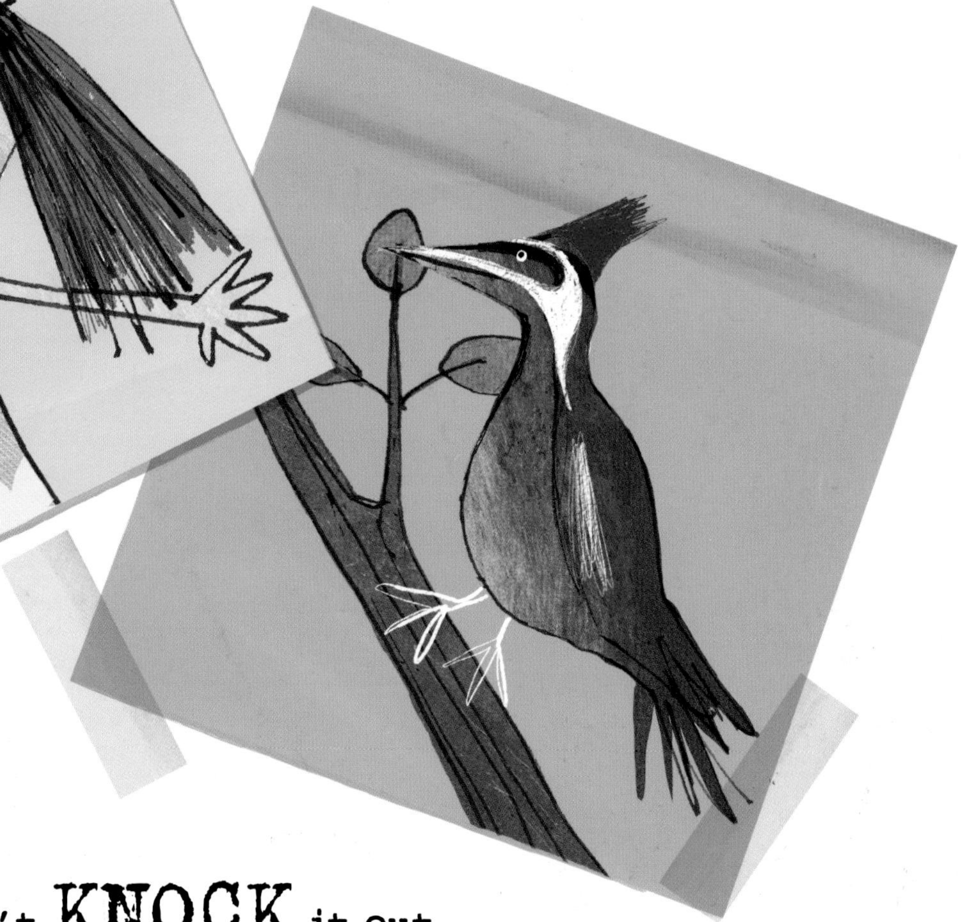

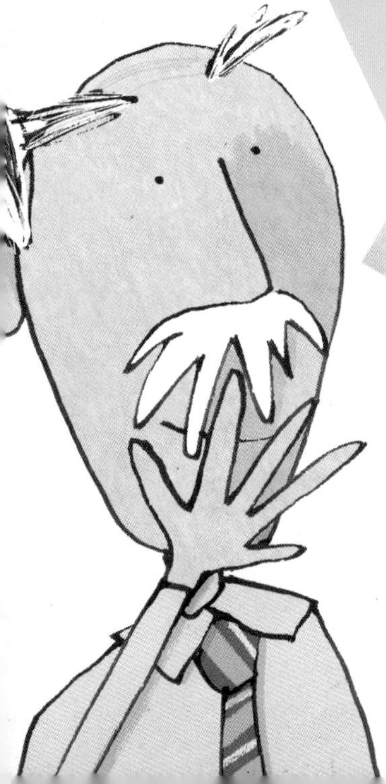

and we can't **KNOCK** it out ...

maybe we can **SUCK** it out. We'll find the biggest elephant and use his trunk, just like a vacuum cleaner, and

WHOOSH...

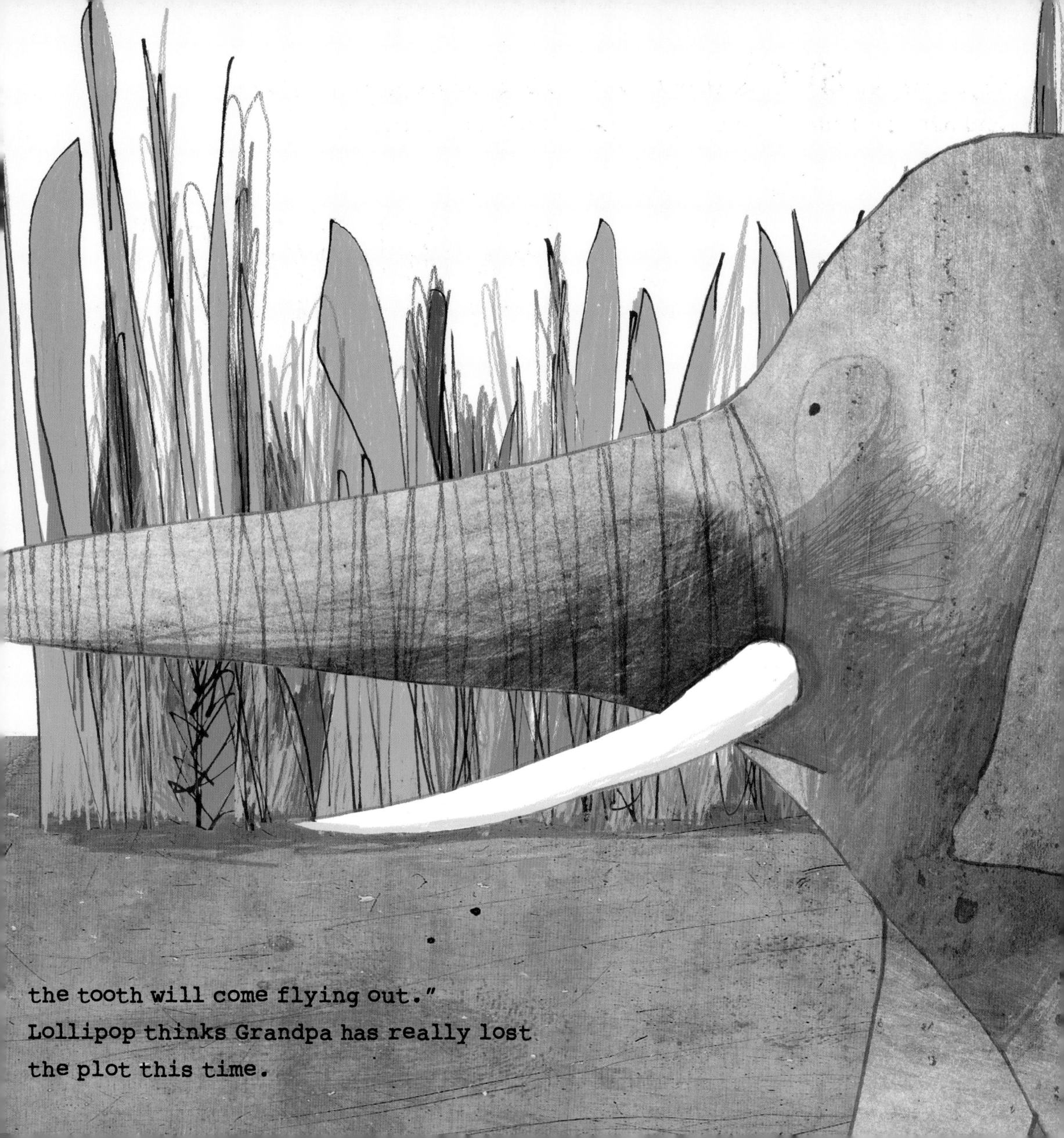

the tooth will come flying out."
Lollipop thinks Grandpa has really lost
the plot this time.

"B-but what happens if the elephant sucks too hard, and I go

WHOOSH

straight up his trunk too?"

"Then," says Grandpa, "I have
completely run out of ideas.
Perhaps we should have a snack and a
rest, and come up with a better plan."

Lollipop chooses a big, red, shiny apple.
She opens her mouth wide and takes an enormous bite.

CRUNCH!

Lollipop feels a **wibble**...

then a **wobble**, and then...

"It's out, it's out!" shouts Lollipop,
and she dances in a circle around the kitchen.

Suddenly, she stops,
and runs her tongue
over the place where
the wobbly tooth used
to be.
She can feel a
GINORMOUS gap.

Luckily, Grandpa knows
just what to do.

"We're going straight
to the dentist, Lollipop.
He knows all about
wobbly teeth and
GINORMOUS gaps."

The dentist's waiting room smells funny and is VERY quiet.

"You must be Lollipop," says the dentist.
"I'm Mr McCavity, and I hear you have some splendid teeth."

"My wobbly tooth came out," explains Lollipop,
showing Mr McCavity her gap.

Mr McCavity says to Lollipop,

"You'd better hop onto my chair so that I can take a good look."

The chair tilts backwards with a

ZZZZZZuuuuuuurrrrrr,

until Lollipop is lying on her back and staring

into a big bright light.

Mr McCavity's head appears in front of the light.
Lollipop can see right up his nose.
It's very hairy.

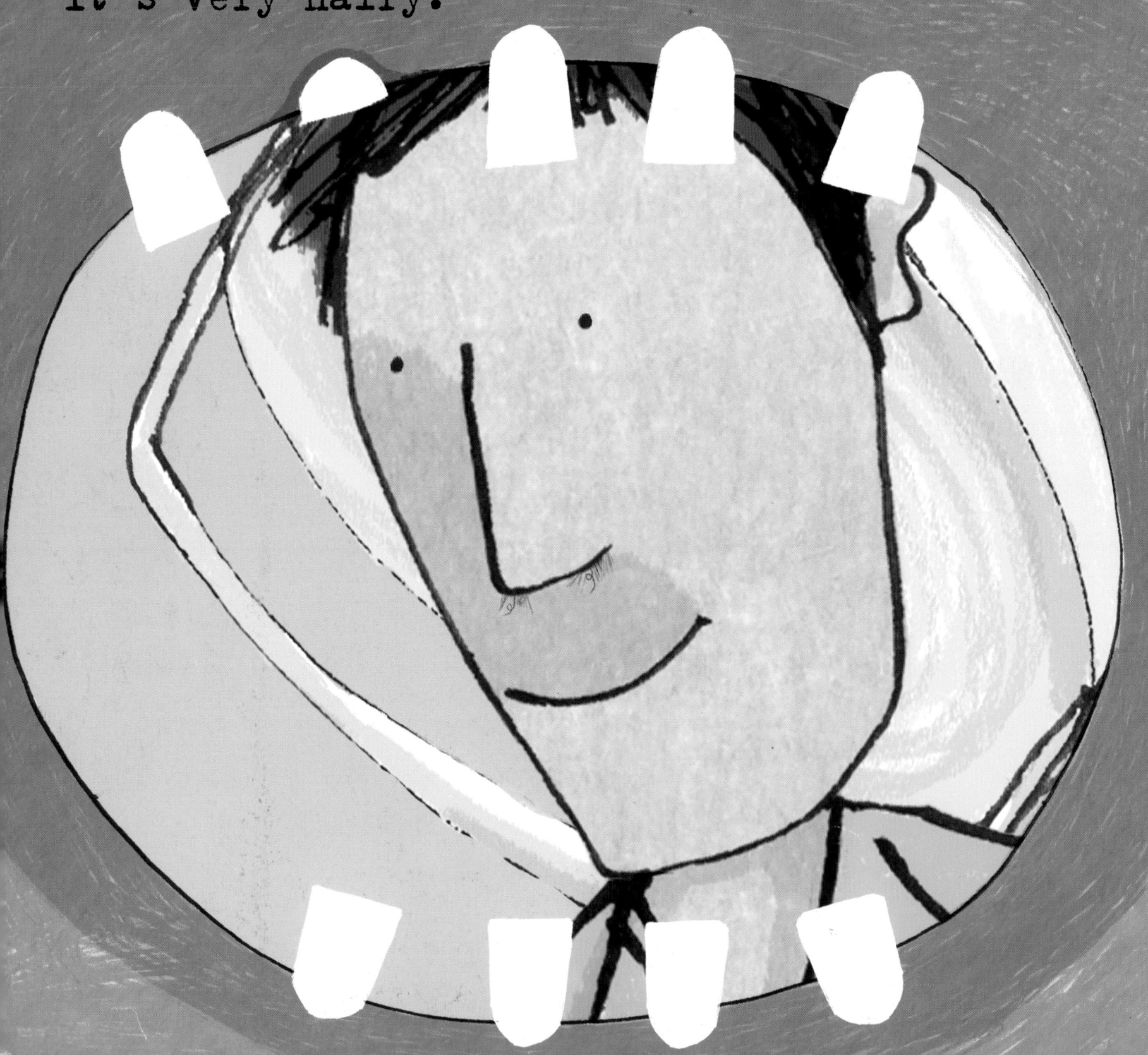

"Open wide," says Mr McCavity, and Lollipop opens her mouth
wider than it has ever gone before.
"AHA!" says Mr McCavity.
"There's already a brand new tooth waiting to fill that gap."
He holds up a little mirror so that Lollipop can see.

Lollipop slides off the big chair.

WHEEEEEEEEEEEEEEEEE!

The dentist lets her choose
a sticker to put on her dress.

Lollipop grins a gappy, gummy smile.

"Now I look just like Grandpa," she says.

Lollipop and Grandpa go home just in time for lunch.